To all of my friends, who are the best friends in the whole wide world —T. H.

This edition published in Great Britain in 2009 by Boxer Books Limited.
www.boxerbooks.com

First published in the U.S. in 2007 by Schwartz & Wade Books, an imprint of Random House Children's Books.
Published by arrangement with Random House Children's Books, a division of Random House, Inc. New York, New York, U.S.A.
All rights reserved.

A CIP catalogue record for this book is available from the British Library upon request.

ISBN 13: 978-1-906250-32-4

1 3 5 7 9 10 8 6 4 2

Printed in China

All of our papers are sourced from managed forests and renewable resources.

Duck, Duck, Goose

written & illustrated by Tad Hills

Boxer Books

Goose stood very still. He did not want to disturb the butterfly on his head.

Just wait until Duck gets a look at this, he thought.

"Bluebird, have you seen Duck?" he asked carefully.

"He's approaching from the west," said Bluebird. "And he's not alone."

"Not alone?" honked Goose. "And where's west?"

"That-a-way," Bluebird pointed and was gone.

Just wait until Goose meets Thistle, Duck thought as he raced his new friend across the meadow.

Along the way, he shouted out all his and Goose's favourite spots. "There's the lily pond and the shady thicket. Up ahead are the puddles by the river."

"Oh! I love puddles!" Thistle yelled, and ran ahead.

"Wow, you sure are one fast duck," Duck called after her.
"I sure am! I'm probably the fastest duck in the whole
wide world," the little duck boasted.

Just then Goose heard twigs snap and leaves rustle. He watched his butterfly flutter away.

Out of the bushes came Duck and Thistle.

"You missed it, Duck," said Goose. "A butterfly was sitting on my head."

"Exciting news, Goose," said Duck.

"Are you sure it wasn't a moth?" Thistle asked.

"Oh, yes, I'm sure, little duck," Goose said.

"I'm not little!"
Thistle shouted.

"Goose, meet Thistle," Duck said.

"Nice to meet you, Thistle," Goose honked. "How long is she staying?" he whispered to Duck.

"Forever," said Duck happily. "She just moved here."

"You know, Duck," Thistle said, "once, THREE butterflies landed on my head at the same time!" She leapt in the air.

"Three butterflies, all at the same time! Isn't Thistle amazing, Goose?" Duck quacked.

"Yeah, she's something, all right."

"That's two more butterflies than you had!" said Duck.

"I know, I can add up," mumbled Goose.

"Hey, I'm really good at maths, too!" exclaimed Thistle. "I'm probably the best!"

"For example, what's four plus nine, Goose?" she asked. "Think fast!" And she kicked a puddle. SPLASH!

"THIRTEEN!" she yelled before Goose could answer. "What about six plus three?" SPLASH! SPLASH!

"NINE, that's easy!" Thistle shouted. "What about seven plus two?" SPLASH! SPLASH! SPLASH! "Nine again, of course!" Thistle screamed. "Nine, nine, nine, nine!"

"I can't do maths when I'm being splashed," sputtered Goose.
"Can we please play something else?"

"I can hold my breath practically forever," boasted Thistle. "Can you, Goose?"

"Do I have to?"

"Oh, come on, it'll be fun," quacked Duck. "I'll time you."

"Fine," said Goose, and he took a big breath.

So did Thistle.

Duck counted. "One hippopotamus, two hippopotamus . . ." all the way to eleven, when Goose collapsed.

"I win!" said Thistle, doing a little spin.

"You are so good at that! I bet you really could have lasted forever!" exclaimed Duck.

"I'd like to see her try," groaned Goose.

"So what else do you do around here for fun?" quacked Thistle.
Duck looked at Goose. "We play," he said.

"I bet I'll win,"
quacked Thistle.

"We run around the meadow or kick our ball," said Goose.
"There is no winning."

"Then why bother?" said Thistle. "Last one to the top of
the hill is a rotten egg." And off she ran.

"Well, I guess I'm the rotten egg," Goose said.

"Come on, Goose!" Duck yelled. "Let's see how fast Thistle can run downhill."

"Can't we just watch the clouds instead?" honked Goose.

But Thistle and Duck

were too far ahead

to hear him.

At the bottom of the hill, Goose moaned, "Can't we just –"
"Stand on our heads?" Thistle interrupted. "Of course!

But first let's have a
who-can-hop-on-one-
foot-the-longest match,

a walk-across-a-log
challenge,

a balance-a-stick-on-your-head contest,

and a jump-over-a-bush race."

When it was time to stand on their heads, Goose had had enough.

"I'd rather look for butterflies," he said to himself.

"On your marks, get set . . ." Thistle quacked. "Ready, Goose?"

But Goose was nowhere in sight.

"Time me, okay, Duck?" said Thistle.

Duck sighed. "Sure.

One hippopotamus . . . Did Goose say where he was going?

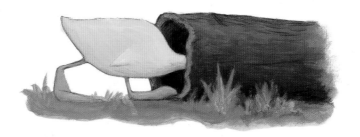

Two hippopotamus . . . Do you think he'll come back?

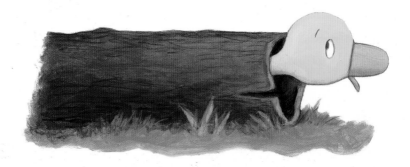

Three hippopotamus . . . Should we go look for him?"

"Who?" squawked Thistle.

"Goose!" squawked Duck.

"Oh, that guy was going to lose anyway. Now let's see if I can beat my personal best. Keep counting."

"What *is* your personal best, Thistle?"

"Three thousand, five hundred and thirteen."

By "six hippopotamus," Duck had had enough.

"I can't believe you're leaving me upside down like this!" cried Thistle as Duck headed off into the tall grass.

Duck looked for Goose in all their favourite places.

But the lily pond
was empty.

The shady thicket
was dark and quiet.

And the river bank felt lonely.

Duck called out to his friend,

"GOOSE!"

but his cry was muffled by

the whir of the wind and

the gurgle of the river.

At last, Duck hung his head and sat down by their favourite bush.

"Oh, Goose, where are you?" he said, wishing that his friend could hear him.

From behind the bush came a familiar honk.

"Goose?" Duck called out.

"DUCK!" answered Goose.

"GOOSE! Where have you been?"

Goose sighed. "I don't like to stand on my head."

"No," said Duck. "Actually, I don't, either."

"And when I hold my breath too long, I get dizzy."

"Me too," said Duck.

"And walking across a log scares me."

Duck looked at Goose. "I thought you did a great job."

"But Thistle won every time," Goose said. "She's very talented."

Duck nodded. "I think she's had lots of practice."

"You know," said Goose, "hopping on one foot is fun for a while, but sometimes I like to sit and smell the flowers."

"Or listen to the river," Duck added.

"Or feel a warm breeze," said Goose.

"Or look for butterflies," quacked Duck.

"Or even kick the ball around the meadow," honked Goose.

"Hey, good idea!" agreed Duck.

Suddenly, out of the tall grass, Thistle appeared. "WOW! You guys are good hiders!" she quacked.

"And you're a good finder," said Goose.

"What shall we do now?" asked Thistle.

"I think it's time for a nap," Goose said.

Duck pretended to yawn. "I bet I can fall asleep faster than anyone."

"Not faster than me," Goose said.

"I'M the fastest faller-asleeper ever!" Thistle bragged.

"Okay," said Goose. "Whoever falls asleep first
and sleeps the longest –"

"Is the all-time best –" Duck quacked.

"CHAMPION NAPPER –" Goose honked.

"In the whole wide world!"

shouted Thistle.

And luckily for Duck and Goose, Thistle was.

Other Boxer Books paperbacks

Duck & Goose: Tad Hills

Duck and Goose find an egg. "Who does it belong to?" they ask. Parents everywhere will recognise this tale of one-upmanship, which firmly establishes the positive aspects of learning to share.

ISBN 13: 978-1-905417-26-1

Fine As We Are: Algy Craig Hall

Fine As We Are is an exquisitely illustrated story of sibling rivalry. Little Frog is living happily with his mum until the arrival of a multitude of little brothers and sisters. How will Little Frog cope?

ISBN 13: 978-1-905417-74-2

Grumpy Cat: Britta Teckentrup

Cat likes being alone, but a cuddly kitten snuggles up to him and begins to follow him everywhere. At first, Cat tries to shake him off. But when Kitten is in danger, this grumpy cat's true nature is revealed.

ISBN 13: 978-1-905417-70-4

Mr Follycule's Wonderful Beard: H.L. Goldsworthy & Georgie Birkett

Mr Follycule wishes for a beard to take care of and is amazed when his wish comes true. The trouble is, his wonderful beard won't stop growing! A hilarious tale of an ordinary wish with an extraordinary outcome.

ISBN 13: 978-1-906250-43-0